Duckie Goosie

Fixes His Roof

BY LANDEN AND LANCE SANDERS

DRAWINGS BY LYNN WADE

For DeGalynn Wade Sanders,
for her love and vision.
This book would not be possible
without my nana, my papa, and Aunt V.

1

This is Duckie Goosie.

2

This is Duckie Goosie's home.

3

When it rained, Duckie Goosie's roof leaked.

4

Duckie Goosie needed a new roof.

5

So Duckie Goosie ordered everything he needed for a new roof: roofing paper, a staple gun, staples, a hammer, shingles, nails, and a ladder.

6

Before Duckie Goosie could build a new roof, he carefully removed the old roof. Duckie Goosie used a tarp to protect his yard and collect the old shingles and roofing paper to be recycled.

7

Fixing a roof is hard work.
First you unroll the roofing paper …

8

Then you staple it down.

9

Next, you pull the plastic strip off the top of the shingle …

Put it in place and nail it down.

Just as Duckie Goosie was pulling the plastic off a shingle, a strong wind blew it out of his hand.

The plastic strip danced in the breeze.
The sun made it shine just like a rainbow.

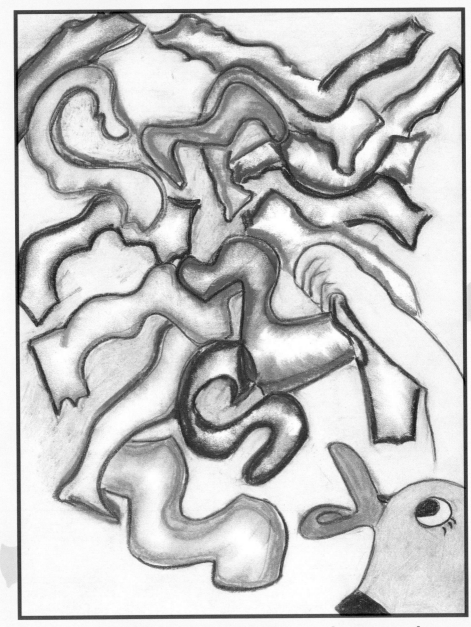

13

Instead of placing the plastic strips in bags to be recycled, Duckie Goosie decided to let the wind blow all the plastic strips high up in the air.

14

"Watch them fly! Watch them fly!"
Duckie Goosie shouted.

It takes a lot of shingles to cover a roof, but finally Duckie Goosie was finished. Duckie Goosie was proud of his new roof.

When Duckie Goosie climbed down from the roof, Duckie Goosie saw his neighbor, Monkey Doggie, and Monkey Doggie was very cross.

All the plastic strips from Duckie Goosie's roof covered Monkey Doggie's yard. What a mess!

18

Duckie Goosie apologized for the mess and started cleaning it up right away.

19

Duckie Goosie was sad. Cleaning up Monkey Doggie's yard was hard work. Duckie Goosie had fun watching the plastic strips fly away, but he did not think about where they all went.

20

Monkey Doggie saw how hard Duckie Goosie was working to clean up the mess. Monkey Doggie felt bad for being so upset with Duckie Goosie.

21

Monkey Doggie decided to help Duckie Goosie. With the two of them working together, they were finished in no time.

22

To celebrate their hard work, Duckie Goosie and Monkey Doggie shared banana bread and bubble cream juice.

23

Duckie Goosie was proud of the work he had done, but was really proud of the new friendship he made with his neighbor.

24

THE END.

LANDEN

&

Lance Sanders

Landen and Lance Sanders
hatch another Duckie Goosie tale.